The Cardboard Box and Me

Mary Anderson Moody

Fulton Books, Inc.
Meadville, PA

Published by Fulton Books 2020

ISBN 978-1-64654-735-7 (paperback)
ISBN 978-1-63710-551-1 (hardcover)
ISBN 978-1-64654-736-4 (digital)

Printed in the United States of America

"The Cardboard Box And Me" is dedicated to my grandchildren—Graham, Eliza, Beckham, McClure, Emily and Liam—all of whom have played in cardboard boxes, and to my husband, Bert, for his encouragement and love.

On Monday, a new refrigerator arrived in a cardboard box. The fridge went in; the box stayed out. I peeked at the trashman on his route. Do you think that he saw me?

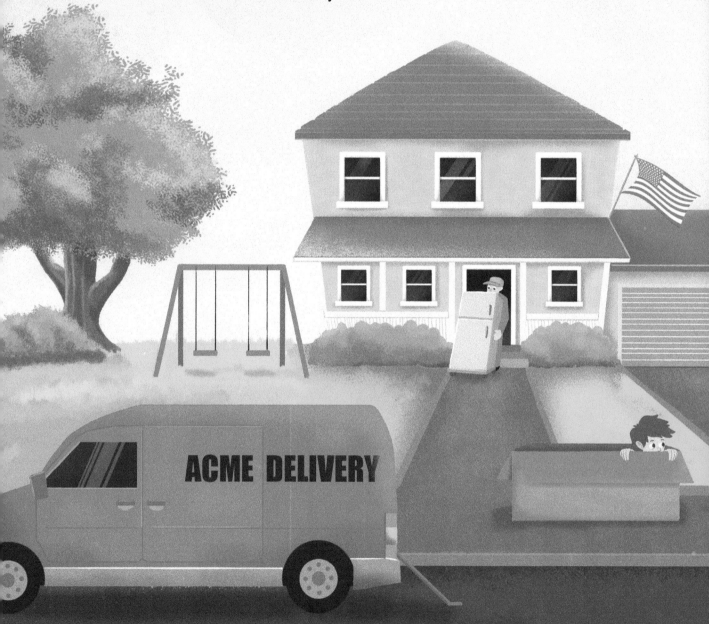

1

At the end of the day, I put the box away. "See you tomorrow," I say.

Mom likes the new refrigerator. I like the cardboard box.

On Tuesday, the cardboard box became a fast race car. I revved the motor. *Vroom*! *Vroom*! The car ran fine. I raced it to the finish line. Can you guess who won first place? At the end of the day, I put the box away.

"See you tomorrow," I say.

On Wednesday, the cardboard box became a dark bat cave. Bats flew here. Bats flew there. I ran faster than my hair. Can you imagine that? At the end of the day, I put the box away.

"See you tomorrow," I say.

On Thursday, the cardboard box became a helicopter. It made a *womp-womp-womping* sound. I thought it lifted off the ground. Did you see me soaring high on the way up to the sky? At the end of the day, I put the box away.

"See you tomorrow," I say.

My DeLi

9

On Friday, the cardboard box became a take-out deli. I cooked mud biscuits, french-fried sticks, and a stink bug pie from an insect mix. Does not that sound delicious? At the end of the day, I put the box away.

"See you tomorrow," I say.

On Saturday, the cardboard box became a yellow school bus. I got on the bus, not to be late.

Mom called out, "Wait! Wait! Wait! Do you know what day this is?"

At the end of the day, I put the box away.

"See you tomorrow," I say.

MOM SAYS NO SNAKES
PET SHOW TODAY 10¢

On Sunday, the cardboard box became a pet show stage. Each neighbor paid a dime to see each other's pet act neighborly.

Lightning showed up uninvited. Thunder made the pets excited.

Dogs barked, "*Woof!*" Birds screeched, "*Screeech!*" Cats meowed "*Meeoow!*" hysterically. Friends ran home, except for me. I was already there, you see.

All night long, the wind blew hard. Something tumbled across the yard. I almost opened my eyes to peep, but one wink later, I was back asleep.

SH
ICE

PET SHOW
TODAY 10¢
MOM SAYS NO SNAKES

On Monday morning when I woke up, the cardboard box was gone—the race car, the dark bat cave, the helicopter, the take-out deli, the yellow school bus, the pet show stage. I thought about the refrigerator. Had it disappeared as well? I ran into the kitchen. The fridge was there, but the cardboard box had gone somewhere. How could a whole week of play disappear in just one day?

Did I put the box away at the end of yesterday? I went outside to think a bit. All the clues began to fit. The biggest clue fell off the truck. How is that for super luck?

MOM SAYS NO SNAKES
PET SHOW TODAY!

I had solved the mystery! The cardboard box came back to me. Welcome home, cardboard box! Mom likes the new refrigerator. I like the cardboard box.

About the Author

Mary Moody graduated from the University of Georgia in elementary education and was a member of the Alpha Delta Pi sorority. She has taught primary grades in both public and private schools. Before her retirement, she served as director and teacher of the preschool and kindergarten programs at the First Baptist Church in Augusta, Georgia. *The Cardboard Box and Me* was awarded first place in children's literature at the regional Sand Hills Writers Conference sponsored by Augusta University. Mary enjoys writing children's stories and composing piano music. She and her husband live in Augusta, Georgia.

CPSIA information can be obtained
at www.ICGtesting.com
Printed in the USA
BVHW020850291121
622770BV00005B/150